:01
First Second
New York

Chapter 1

THE PRINCE IS HOLDING A BALL!!
"Countess Clementine of Artois is pleased to host the summer residency of her nephew, the Crown Prince Sebastian of Belgium, at her Paris estate."
All eligible young women are invited to attend the Royal Spring Ball celebrating the Prince's 16th birthday.
His Highness looks forward to making your lovely acquaintances.

"After all, Paris is the city of love."
SQUEEEAAL!!

Retouches
Couture
Can I help you, madame?
Do you have time to make a new dress for tomorrow? It's urgent. We've been to five tailors today and every one of them turned us away.
I take it the young lady is going to the ball?

Hrmph!
If I can help it. She absolutely ruined her gown last night by going riding in the woods! RIDING!
SOMEONE forgot to pack my riding clothes!
Lady Sophia, if you so much as utter another word—
I'll see what I can do. We're extremely busy, as you can see, but my seamstresses are the best in town.
We'll try to have something for you by tomorrow morning.
Who's available? FRANCES.
Come measure the young lady.

I assure you I hate this as much as you do.
Would the lady like her dress identical to the old one or completely new?
Whatever. You know what, just make it ghastly. Make me look like the devil's wench.
You sure you'll be all right, Frances?

Yes.
My eyes are a little sore, but I'll be fine.

Suit yourself. Don't work too hard. This job won't love you back, you know.

Presenting Lady Adelina Tonnerre, daughter of Count Tonnerre!

My Imogene spent four hours with the hairdresser this morning. Of her own volition! Last year I couldn't get her to brush her hair!
Oh, they grow up so fast. When my Delilah left the house today, my husband nearly cried. Imagine, the Archduke of Austria, crying!
Well I brought all four of my daughters. I figure one of them will be sloppy enough to bag the prince.
Presenting Lady Sophia Rohan!
SWING

"AN ABOMINATION OF TASTE AND DISTINCTION!!"
That's what they're saying about us! Do you understand? When I say "us," that is MY reputation on the line.
Frances, these people have the power to RUIN us.
I'm sorry! I was just giving the client what she wanted.
What SHE wanted—?!
...
Frances, my girl. The client is not the one who wears the dress.
THE CLIENT IS THE ONE WHO PAYS.
Sir, someone's here!

Pardon my interruption.
I heard you're the tailor Lady Sophia Rohan commissioned this dress from?
I, um, yes! The Lady Rohan was at my shop, b-but it was this girl who made the dress! Just a low-level seamstress.
I was so busy the other day, I made the mistake of assigning her!
I see.
It's funny, you see, I was JUST in the process of letting her go.

Is that so. In that case, my lady, I represent a client who would like to hire you as a personal seamstress.
The offer is three francs a week. Are you interested?
WHAT?
The client was very impressed with your work and insisted I come today before anyone else made an offer.
Well, ah, I think there's been a misunderstanding! When I said letting her go, I meant promoting her to head seamstress!
Frances, m'dear, why don't I raise your wage to four francs a week!
Five francs.

FIVE?? I'll make you a designer!
No. I quit.
Tell your client I accept the offer.
Very good. I'll arrange for your transport immediately.
Where am I going?
Be ready for pickup early tomorrow morning.

I have to pack!

Chapter 2

My name is Emile. If you need anything, please let me know.
Emile, may I ask? Is the client an aristocrat?
The client is very distinguished indeed.

What's this for?
Put this on.
The client asks for privacy.

SHUT
Come forward. Don't be afraid.
Are you the client?
Yes. Please come forward. Don't be shy.

What's your name?
Frances. Why am I not allowed to see you?
I...I had an accident when I was younger. I'm embarrassed to show my face.
Are you a princess?
Yes. More or less.
Forgive me, Your Highness. If I'm going to make clothes for you, I have to be able to see you. I won't judge you, I promise.
Hmmm. You're right. Okay, just a second.

Okay,
now you
can look.

Your Highness.
No, no, please, Frances! Don't be so formal. Make yourself comfortable!
Here, have some candy.
Thank you. This is such an honor. I'm not sure how I ended up here.
Are you kidding me? I was at that ball. When I saw the dress you made for Lady Sophia, I thought, "She's the one. She's the one I want to make dresses for me."

What style of dress are you looking for?
Beauty. Drama. Romance. Anything you think is beautiful.
When I walk into a room, I want everyone to notice.
They don't have to love it, or understand it, but they're going to remember it.
Here, let me show you some stuff...

These are...
This dress was worn by Lady Augustina Stuart on her wedding day, inspired by her husband's frequent trips to India. Just look at the detailing on the sleeves.
This is a design from Charles Bedouin's "Arabian Nights" operetta!
And these are by Marie Hofhansolva for the Russian Ballet!
Look at her shoes!

Oh, I have a pair just like those.
Here! You have to try 'em on.
I can't.
C'mon!
I'm going to fall!
No you won't, you're doing fine—
AAH!

AAAAAHHHHHH!!
YOUR HIGHNESS!

PRINCE SEBASTIAN!
Are you all right?
Yes, I am. What's the trouble?
We heard screams.
Prince...

Oh!
Ha-ha-ha! It was nothing. I stubbed my toe here and—
EEEEK!
Well then. Pardon our intrusion. We'll leave you to your privacy.
...
I told you it was the prince.

You're a boy.
You're the prince.
I'm so sorry. Please don't tell anyone about this.
I'm the king's only son. If anybody found out the prince wore dresses, it would ruin the whole family.
My parents would disown me and my life would be over. My father would... my father...

This isn't a joke, then. You really wanted me to make dresses for you.
I wouldn't lie about that.
Look, I'm sorry. I'll send for a carriage right away.
Take anything you want, just please don't tell anyone.
Here—
I'm not going anywhere.
I quit working for that unpleasant tailor so I could design dresses for you, the Crown Prince.
Why would I want to go back?

You're not weirded out?
What difference does it make? This is my dream job.
We can help each other.
You keep my secret and continue to make beautiful clothes for me...
...And I may someday be a great designer.

Deal.

You will live here with the other servants. When you're finished, the prince will see you in his private dressing room.
This is the key to the dressing room. Keep it safe. The only other copies belong to the prince and myself.
Do you...
I know everything about the prince. It is none of my business.

You said you want this dress to be fruit-jam inspired?
Yes! Think marmalades and preserves.
And you want it in two days? What for?
You'll see. I just got that wig and I need something that will go with it perfectly.

Can I ask?
Why do you wear girl clothes?
I don't know.
Some days I look at myself in the mirror and think, "That's me, Prince Sebastian! I wear boy clothes and look like my father."
Other days it doesn't feel right at all.
Those days I feel like I'm actually...
...a princess.

What made you want to be a designer?
The first time I came to the city, I came with my mother to deliver goods for her employer.
When we passed the Grand Music Hall, I saw a poster for a ballet called "The Muse of Crystallia."
THE MUS
CRYS
I couldn't stop looking at it. For weeks afterward I kept drawing versions of that poster, trying to imagine what the costumes really looked like.

Eventually I stopped drawing Crystallia and just started making up costumes for my own imaginary ballets.
At some point I realized this was a real job somebody had and I wanted to be that person. The person who makes beautiful things.
What do you think of this?

You want to know what I think? I think it's too conservative.
It's elegant.
But you don't do elegant! You like fantasy, you like drama!
I just don't want you to look silly. What about those other dresses in your closet?
Those are my MOTHER'S dresses. Frances, you being here is the start of something new for me.
My whole life is other people deciding what's acceptable. When I put on a dress, I get to decide what's silly.

Okay.

Okay.

What do you think?
...This is incredible! You look amazing!
Good.
Okay, grab your coat. We're going out.
Out?
Meet me at the side entrance!

MALDON'S PRESERVES
Sebastian, what are we doing here?
Frances, I need to tell you something.

I've never been in public dressed like this before.
No one's ever had to look at me.
And now, ladies and gentlemen, the event of the evening!
The beauty pageant! Who will be crowned Miss Marmalade?
Beauty pageant! Why didn't you tell me?
I didn't think I'd go through with it!
You want to go back?

No. No, I'm going to do this. I just wanted you to know.
Okay, here goes.
SEBASTIAN!
I see a number of lovely ladies out in the crowd tonight. Step right up to the stage, ladies, and show us what you've got!
The rest of you give a huge round of applause for your favorite contestants. The most popular lady of the night goes home with not one, not two, but THREE cases of Maldon's finest preserves and the title of Miss Marmalade!

Ooh, fanning myself over here. That look is springtime in bloom.
"Can't miss me in a crowd," say those horizontal stripes!

Ooh-la-la, here comes a flower of the orient!
Cool and minty fresh, this look will certainly wake you up!

Oh my goodness, a goddess from the land of citrus!

And there we have our winner, ladies and gentlemen! The new Miss Marmalade!
And tell us, miss...
...what is your name?

You can call me...
LADY CRYSTALLIA.

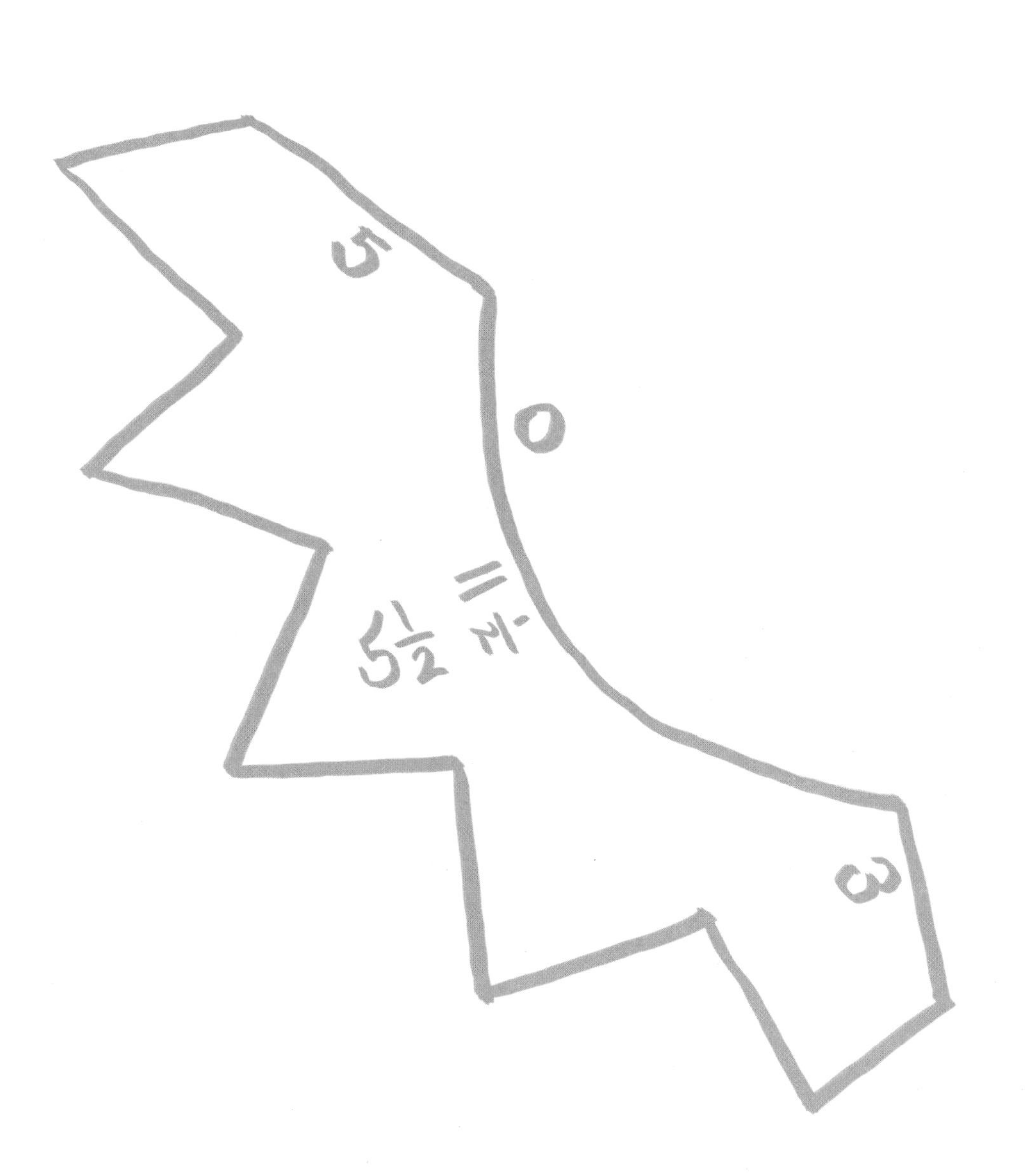

Chapter 3

KNOCK
KNOCK
Your Highness?

Your Highness?
The king and queen request your company. They have important matters to discuss.
Okay, tell them I'm on my way!

BLOCK HIM!! BLOCK HIM!!

YES!
One for Team Leroy! Ha-ha, sorry, lad. You need to cheer harder for your servants.
Ha-ha, yes. Speaking of servants, I hired a new seamstress for myself. Her name's Frances. You might see her around.
Very good. I'm glad you're taking an interest in your appearance!
So, have you given any more thought to the ladies who came to your party the other night?
Oh. Um...
Did you like any of them?

They were all nice. I mean, it's hard to get to know anybody at such a big party, you know?
Your mother and I agree! That's why we've decided to start setting you up on individual meetings—
CUT HIM OFF!! DON'T LET THEM PASS!!
Wait, like here?
Yes!
In fact, tomorrow we're getting a visit from Princess Juliana.
You remember her? We vacationed with her family, the royal family of Monaco, when you were both five!

Princess Juliana is a lovely young lady of fine breeding.
Oh, we would be SO happy if the two of you got along!
But don't you think this is a little fast? I just turned sixteen! I have a whole life ahead of me to find a wife.
I knew I was marrying your mother when I was three years old!
Your aunt Clem married your uncle and moved here to Paris when she was your age!
Rest in peace.
Our parents decided all that. We're giving you a choice!

Sebastian, you're the Crown Prince. Your most important role in life is preserving our family legacy. The sooner we figure out your future, the sooner we can prepare for it.
What's wrong, son? Women make you nervous? It's good you just hired that seamstress! You'll be needing those new threads—
JUST HIT THE BALL!!
DON'T LET 'EM BLOODY GET AWAY WITH IT!!

What's wrong?
Did you know my father is a military leader?
And his father? And his father's father? How am I supposed to live up to that?
How can someone like me marry a princess? What happens if she discovers who I really am?

How could I do that to someone's daughter? How could I do that to my parents?
When I saw you last night, something clicked. You really were Lady Crystallia!
It was you, but you were more. Bigger. More amazing.
You were like a goddess version of yourself. It was magic.
You know, I felt it, too!
Something about wearing your dress transformed me.

You have it in you, Sebastian. I saw it last night.
It's the first time I felt worthy of all this.
It's weird, I don't feel like Prince Sebastian could lead a nation into battle, but Lady Crystallia could.

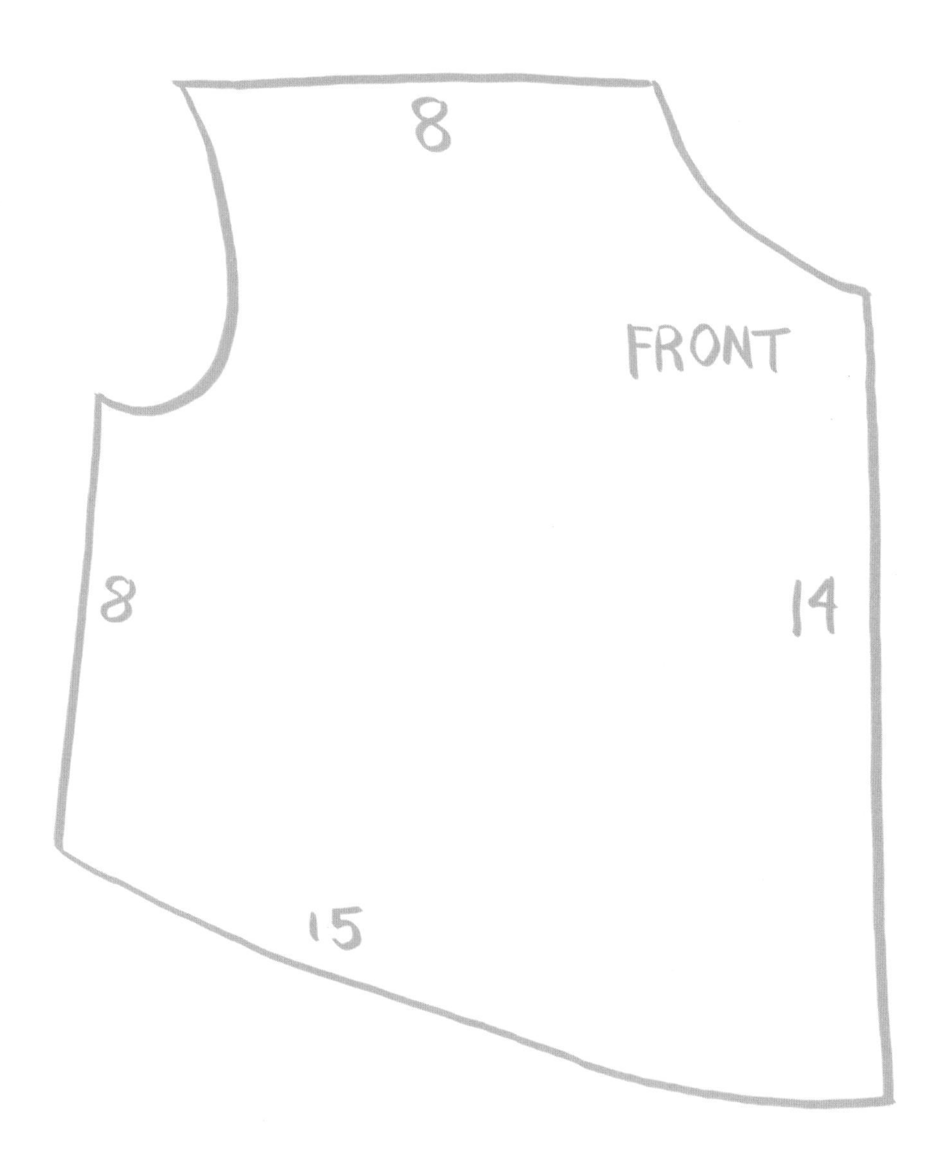

Chapter 4

So you and your brother Marcel have been enjoying your trip to France, Juliana?
Oh, Paris has been so lovely! Your gardens are just exquisite. My brother has quite enjoyed the hunting.
Good ducks.
Maybe Sebastian would like to come out with me and the boys next time.
Looking at all these princesses makes a guy want to blow off a little steam, right?

How is your summer in Paris going, Prince Sebastian?
Oh, uh, wonderful! I've been reading a lot of books...
...eating a lot of... pastries?
Sebastian, why don't you invite Juliana on a tour of the gardens here?
Huh? Oh.
Oh, I would love that! If that's all right with you.
It would be my pleasure.
Make sure Sebastian gives you a tour of the rose garden.
It's quite the retreat for lovers.

It's so beautiful here. Thank you and your family for inviting us.
No, no, I'm glad you're having a good time.
I know why they've brought us here. My parents have been putting a lot of pressure on me, too.
Yeah, sorry about that. I didn't mean for my father to embarrass you. He's really fixated on this betrothal thing.

But this has actually been really nice!
Oh?
Sebastian. I hope this doesn't sound strange, but I like you.
I've met a couple princes now and you're just... You're not like anyone else.
You're sweet, you're considerate. You listen to people...
Well, I'm no Prince Marcel, that's for sure.
HA-HA-HA!

I'm just saying that I would like to continue getting to know you. And maybe over time, if things keep going well...
Maybe we could really think about becoming...
Are you all right, Sebastian?
Oof, I'm not feeling too good. It might be something I ate at dinner. I think I need to go.

The dining room is back toward your right, please don't get lost!

Ha-ha!

CREAK
SLAM
Sebastian...?
I need to go out in that right now.

Look at the waistlines. I bet they're not wearing corsets.
I sure hope not! You really get to focus on the athleticism of the dancers.
Urrgh.
Wow, are you a performer here? How do I get you to come sit with me?
Sorry, sir, I'm...

That's a pretty dress you're wearing.
Thank you. She made it! My seamstress!
And mmm! What's this perfume?

Hey! Do you realize who I am? I own half the electricity in Paris!
We should go.
I'll have you both thrown out of here!
No need.
These ladies are with me.

Peter, these are your friends?
Why don't you come with me.
Yes, I'm very sorry, Mr. DeFreines. We'll be out of your way.

Who you got with you, Peter?
Just some new friends, Pop!

That was close. Mr. DeFreines is not the smoothest drunk, but he's a very important investor.
Oh, didn't mean to be rude. I'm Peter Trippley.
Lady Crystallia.
Pleasure to meet you, miss.
This is Frances, my seamstress. She made this dress.

Quite the find.
No need to thank me. I'm just looking out for kindred spirits.
I noticed how extraordinarily well-tailored Lady Crystallia's dress is, and I couldn't help overhearing you talking about...
Thank you for helping us.
...clothing. As you can see, I'm quite a fan of luxury threads.
That's beautiful work.
YOUR work is beautiful, Frances. Imagine what you could do with a little editing.
Editing?

Yes.
I have to say the aesthetic is not to my taste, but your design skills are undeniable!
I see great things for your future.
Oh.
Thank you.
That man over there is my father, George Trippley. He's opening a new department store in the city, so he's over there buttering up investors.
Wait, I've heard of this. Trippley's, right? It's going to be one of the biggest department stores ever!

Yes, Trippley's! It's going to have everything: furniture, clothing, jewelry. No article of decor or attire you won't be able to find.
That's incredible.
My interest in fashion has inspired my father to make it the central part of his business.
He wants Trippley's to be the leading destination in Paris, and he plans to host a big show at the opening. All the biggest names in fashion will be there.
TRIPPLEY'S
You should come. I'll introduce you to some people.

Can you believe we met the owner of Trippley's?!
Sebastian, you know what this means?
Hmmm...?
We'll be meeting the biggest names in fashion. My work could get discovered!
That'd be amazing. Wasn't Peter kind of critical of you, though?
Yes. But he hasn't seen enough. I just need to convince him.

I need to design a collection.
Something that's gonna make people want to look just like you...

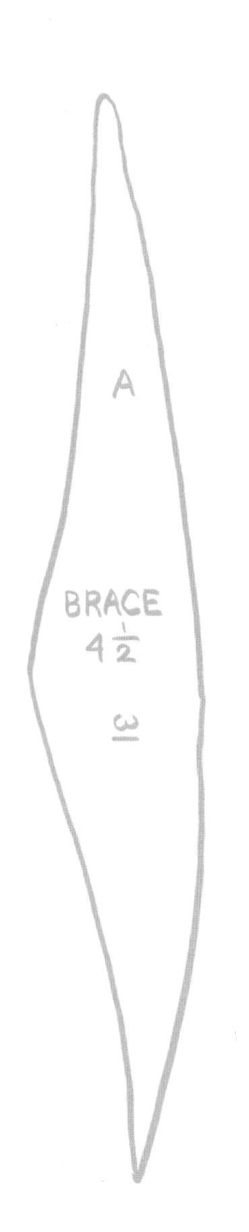

Chapter 5

Sebastian?

I asked if you would like to meet with Princess Lilian this week?
Oh sorry! Yes!
What's gotten into you lately, son? You're barely awake for anything. Are you all right?
Not really. Maybe it's just a lot of stress.

You poor dear. Maybe you could take a little vacation this weekend? Visit the spa town and get some rest and fresh air.
Hey. That sounds great, actually! That's exactly what I need. I'm going to bring Emile and Frances!
Now hold on! What about your meetings?
Oh Leroy, it's just a weekend. Look at him!
Hrmph. Well, prepare to get your lady groove on when you get back, because I'm booking double.

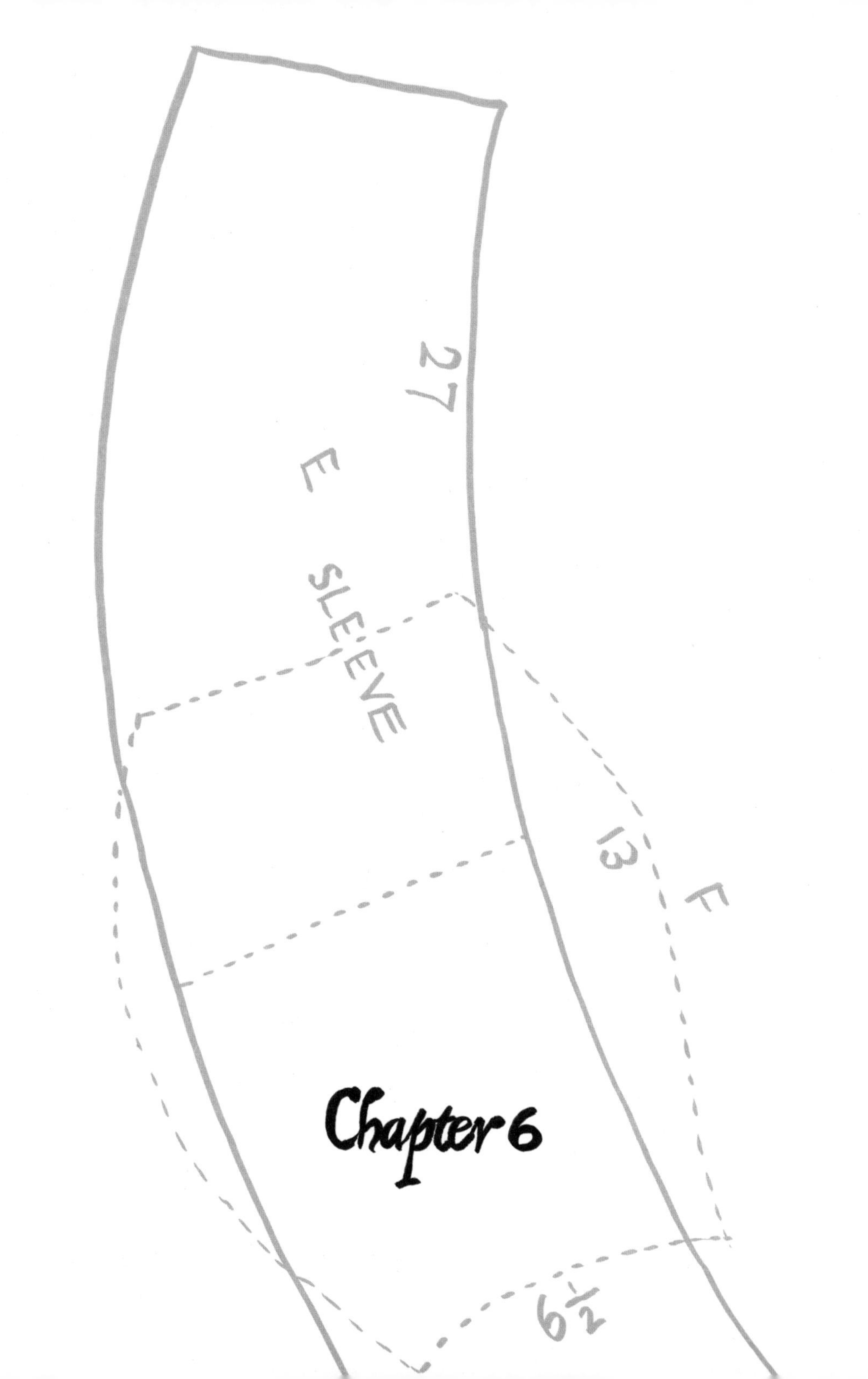

Chapter 6

They're copying me and there's nothing I can do about it.
That's fashion for you. Everyone just wants to hop on the latest trend.
I know, it just bothers me I'm not getting credit for it.
It'll come back to you, I promise.

Oh my
God!

...

Are you the Lady Crystallia?
Oh my goodness, I've heard so much about you! I can't believe I'm meeting you here! I'm Princess Juliana of Monaco.
Pleased to meet you, Princess.
And I'm Prince Marcel. Pleasure.

You are such an inspiration to me and my girl-friends. Your style, and the way you carry yourself.
Thank you. That's very kind.
How are you enjoying the town? Any plans?
Oh just, you know, seeing the sights!
Why don't you join me at the spa today? I'm meeting with Madame Aurelia, who's a personal friend of the family.

Do you know her?
Seb— Crystallia!
She's a costume designer for the Paris Ballet. I'm sure she'd love to meet you!
Can I join the party?
Sorry. This date is ladies only.
One moment, please!

Madame Aurelia designed "The Muse of Crystallia!" You HAVE to go!
Are you kidding me?! My name is LADY Crystallia! She's gonna think I'm a crazy person!
Also, we are going to a SPA and we are going to be wearing very little clothing, oh my God!
Just say you're a fan. She'll understand! Please! This means every-thing to me!
HRRR-NGGGHH!
What time are you meeting?

And so I says to her, darling, cut down on the absinthe!
Oh, there she is! Over here, Crystallia!

FOOSH
Oh my. Ha-ha-ha. Not a very good design at all.

You look a little flushed already.
Oh, I'm just sensitive to high temperatures!
Here, I'd like you to meet Madame Aurelia. Madame, this is Lady Crystallia, whom I've been telling you all about.
Hellooo.

Pleasure. Your name is very interesting.
I designed for a ballet by that name once.
I've heard of it! My seamstress is a big fan. Crystallia's like a fond nickname that I decided to keep!
Oh?

Yes! You were a big influence on her, and by association, me!
Well, then I must've done something right. Juliana here can't stop raving about you. You're who the young girls want to look like right now.
So, you're interested in fashion?
Yes! Always! Ever since I could remember.

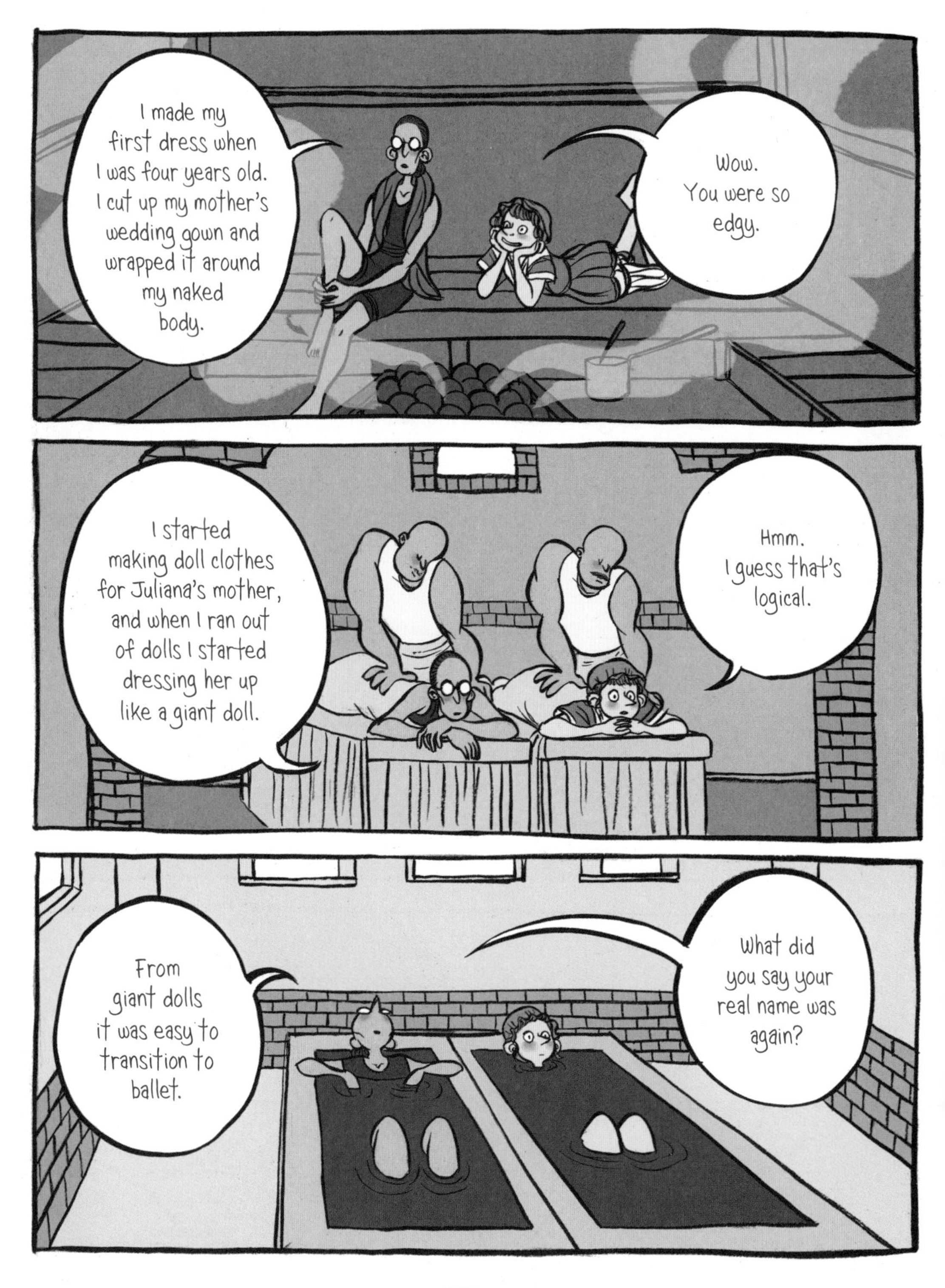
I made my first dress when I was four years old. I cut up my mother's wedding gown and wrapped it around my naked body.
Wow. You were so edgy.
I started making doll clothes for Juliana's mother, and when I ran out of dolls I started dressing her up like a giant doll.
Hmm. I guess that's logical.
From giant dolls it was easy to transition to ballet.
What did you say your real name was again?

...
Nevermind, I'm not going to remember anyway.
Did I mention I'm organizing the fashion show for the department store that's opening in Paris? Trippley's?
No way! I met Peter Trippley.

Really? Why don't you and your seamstress come by the Paris Opera Ballet when you get back in town? Since you say she's a fan.
I could look over her work, see if she has the right stuff for our show.
But no promises.

HOTEL

Frances!
Frances!!
What happened?
She was SO cool. Like scary but in like a totally cool way. Frances, she invited us to the opening of her next ballet.
Us?

Yes, she wants to meet you, and maybe offer you a spot in Trippley's fashion show.
...
What??
No promises, but—
AAAH!
Yes!!
This is crazy! Sebastian! Madame Aurelia wants to meet me! This is a chance of a lifetime and...
...
...And I have to get to work!

Just this once, I think we should celebrate.
What do we do?
Anything! We're on vacation!

No Crystallia tonight?
Thought I'd try wearing one of the outfits you made for Prince Sebastian for a change.
It looks good!

Yeah. It feels good! I actually feel comfortable.
Pardon me, children, but the Ambassador of Prussia is on his way, so if you two could move aside for his carriage...
You fool, it's the Crown Prince Sebastian of Belgium!
Please, Your Highness, come this way.

Plus,
being the prince
can be useful.

It's really working, Sebastian. Every-thing we dreamed of is really happening.
Can you imagine if you never made that dress for Lady Sophia?
I'm sure you would've found someone else.
But there's no one else like you.
It's like nothing can ever stop you. You just keep going.

Everything good that's happened to me has been because of sewing. I'm afraid if I ever stop, I'll be nothing.
You're my friend. If you stopped sewing today you're still the best friend I've ever had.

Well, good night.
Good night, Sebastian.

See you tomorrow.

Chapter 7

Welcome, Princess Louise. It's so nice to see you!
Oh, I'm so excited to spend some time with Prince Sebastian. I haven't stopped thinking about it all week!

Oh, wait just a second. Young lady! Frances, is that your name?
You're Sebastian's seamstress, are you not?
Yes, Your Highness.
Would you mind fixing a tear in one of my garments? My seamstress is out.
Of course!

Lovely! I'll have one of my servants deliver it.
My son has said only wonderful things about you. I hope to see you around a lot!
...blah blah blah blah...
...every-one's always remarking about how you two are such good friends!

I'm actually a champion horse rider back in my country. I've been taking lessons since I was six years old and communing with the horses since I was two.
Some say my stallion, Sir James, is my REAL betrothed.

HAHAHAHAHAHAH
Not to scare you off, Sebastian, but you may have some competition!
What are your favorite hobbies, Prince Sebastian?

Ahem. Sebastian?
Oh. Hobbies. I'm sorry, I don't think I have any that would interest you.
...
...
I'm sorry, I'm not sure I understand.
Does it really matter what my interests are? You're, like, twelve.

Look, I know you came all this way to see me,
but I know we won't have anything in common and this is not going to work.
Sebastian!!
King Leroy, what is this?!
Princess Louise, I'm sorry our parents are making us do this dance.
You seem like a very nice person, and you deserve better than this.

How dare this boy insult my daughter!
I apologize, Queen Caroline. It was very nice to meet you but you'll have to find a different prince. Excuse me.
You ungrateful child...

...
Hrgghh!

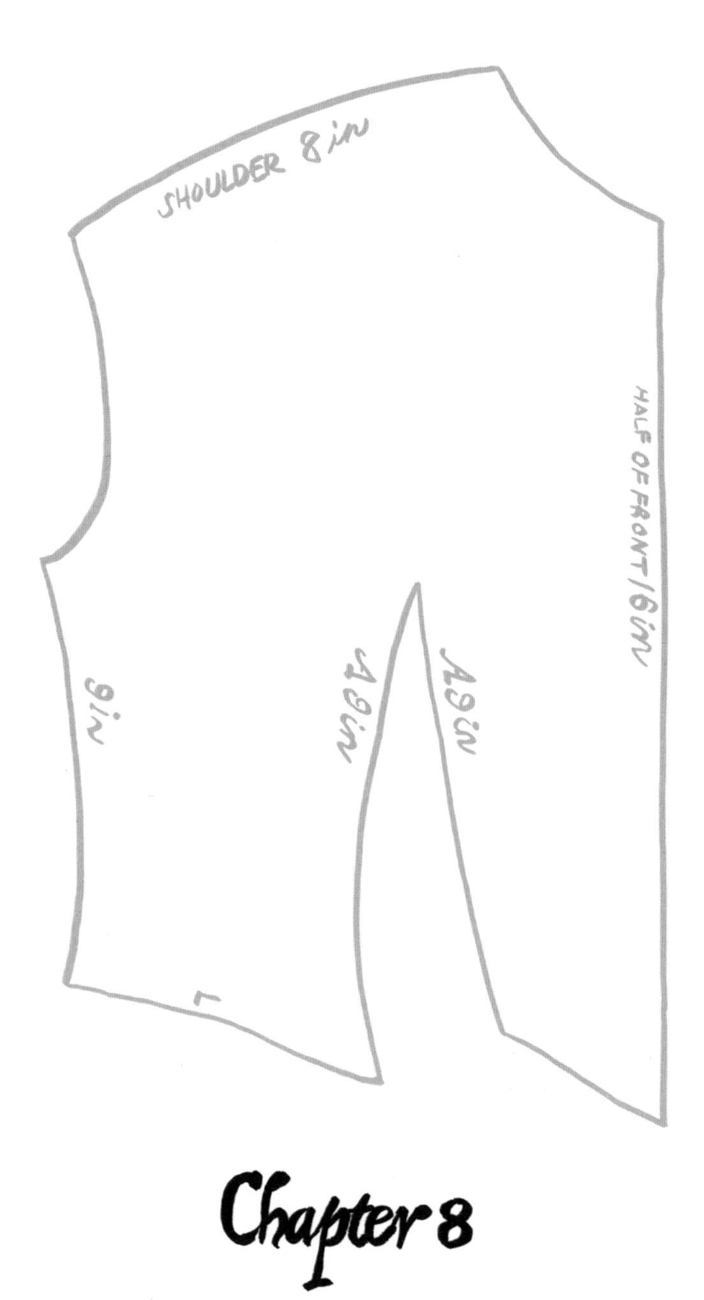

Chapter 8

The surgery is complete. Your father is resting now.

My son...

It must feel like I'm so hard on you all the time. So demanding and critical.
But if anything happened to me, I hope you know that I trust you. I know you'll take good care of your mother. I know you'll take good care of our kingdom.
Father, you don't have to talk like that.
I've been king for a long time.

There's no one else I trust more with everything I'm leaving behind than my own son. Know that.

PARIS BALLET
ADMIT ONE

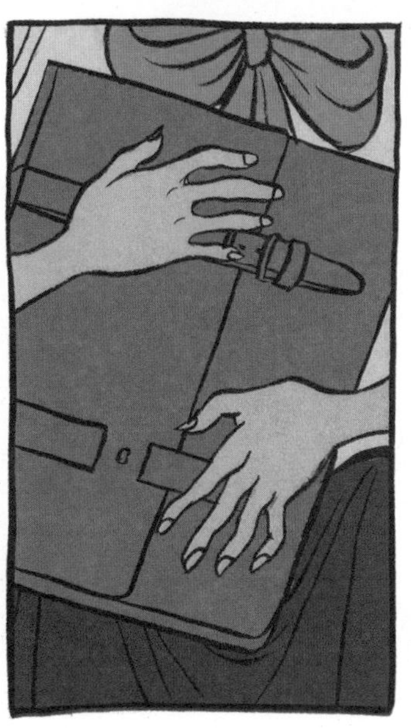

Hey.
I know things have been tough with your father, but I hope you had fun tonight.
He's going to be all right.

Frances. Stop.
I can't let you come with me. I have to see Madame Aurelia alone.
What do you mean?
Everyone knows who you are. My MOTHER knows who you are.
So...
So if everyone finds out the prince's seamstress is also working for Lady Crystallia, they're going to figure out my secret sooner or later!

But why now?
I could be made king any time! If anything happened to my father, that's it for me. I can't take any chances.
What about the show? All the dresses I made?
Don't worry, none of that will change. I'll get your dresses into the show.

Just wait for me back at the palace.
I'll see you there!

I recognize you.

You're friends with Lady Crystallia. I saw you two together in the lobby earlier.
You're Madame Aurelia.

I am. And you are?
No one.

Frances, you're in! You're in the fashion show!

I'm
done.
What?
I can't
do this
anymore.

But you're finally in the show!
What does it matter when I can't even be there?
What if I talked to someone? Are you going to lock me up in a basement to keep me from telling everyone who you are?
Frances, no! Of course not! What are you talking about!
I finally got to meet someone very important to me, and I couldn't even tell her who I was!

Look, I'm sorry about tonight. I wish I'd figured things out sooner.
It doesn't matter! You're a secret, which means I'm a secret! Maybe you can spend the rest of your life living like this, but I can't!
What am I supposed to do?? Do you really think if I tell the world I'm Lady Crystallia everyone's just going to cheer for me?

Wow, we're so excited the new king looks so good in a dress.
Let's celebrate!
I don't know, Sebastian, but I can't help you anymore. I'd rather take my chances starting over than languish in your closet forever.

As your prince, I FORBID you to leave! Return to your servant quarters, now!

You're really leaving.
Good-bye, Sebastian.

Sebastian?
Dearest?

Are you feeling all right? Emile says you haven't eaten since yesterday. Your father and I are worried.
Come on, he doesn't want to be bothered.
Wait, Mother.
I've given it some thought, and I'm ready to propose my betrothal to Princess Juliana.

I've come to accept my responsibilities. I have to grow up so I can one day lead my country.
Are you sure?
Juliana will make a good queen.

Well, this is fantastic news! We'll have to contact the family immediately!
Oh, my son, my son! I can't believe it! We're so happy!

INSIDE OF SLEEVE 10 in
TOP 3 HALF OF SIDE 11in
BOTTOM OF SLEEVE 9 in
B 9 in
C 12 in

Chapter 9

PHILIPE RETOUCHES
LE

Make sure to put all the deliverables to Trippley's in this stack!

Hey, you know that Belgian prince that's been in town for the summer?
He still around? I made ten dresses for his ball. Wish I could've gone.
I hear he just found himself a wife!
No! Who?
Princess Juliana of Monaco!
Oh, she's stunning! I guess if he had to marry someone other than me, it may as well be her.
They're going to make such beautiful babies!

Excuse me.

I'm so sorry. I'll take care of it.

Gentlemen, welcome!
Sorry, we had a little mishap but all your boxes are being packed right now.
No worries. I'll have these gentlemen here help out.

Frances? That you?
Peter. Hi.
Fancy running into you here. Is this what you do during the day when you're not out running with Lady Crystallia?
I'm actually not working for Lady Crystallia anymore.
Huh. Well, that's too bad.

Excuse me, miss! Could I borrow this young lady for a bit?
I need help sorting through some of these items back at the store.
Well...

Thank you!
Come with me.
Where are we going?
To Trippley's!

TRIPPLEY'S

We're almost there. Opening day is less than two weeks away. The whole floor down there is going to be the clothing department.
Wow, Peter, this is incredible. You're going to change the way people buy clothes.
You know, since you're no longer under Crystallia's employment, maybe you'd be interested in working for me.
We're looking to debut some sophisticated women's clothing collections at the show. There's a spot open for you, if you want it.

You want me? I thought you didn't think my work was ready yet.
I've noticed your work trickling down to the streets. You've got the eye. But working for Crystallia kept you from maturing into the artist you needed to be.
I can help you. I think we can do beautiful work together.

My father wants to market this line to the masses. He's a powerful man.
And associating with him can make you very powerful as well.

You are invited to the betrothal ceremony of Prince Sebastian & Princess Juliana On the 14th of April

All alone tonight, miss?

You look sour. Have a drink of this.
What is it?
Just try it. It'll lift your spirits.

Hey. Remember me?

Do I?
I'll give you a hint.
I know, I know, I know who you are. You're Prince Marcel, Juliana's brother.
So I did leave an impression! Did you hear my sister's getting betrothed tomorrow?
Maybe you'd like to come to the party with me.
Too late! This is Lady Crystallia's last night here.
Where are you going?
Disappearing! I'm getting away from this awful place.

Wow. What happened?
Nothing. I did it all to myself. I hurt people. And I'm going to hurt YOU if you're not careful.
I'd like to see you try.
You have nooooo idea, buddy.
Anyway, that's why I have to go now.
Hey, hey, hey, let me at least offer you a ride home.
I can do iiiit!

You know I'm royalty, right?
You'd be very lucky to be on the arm of someone like me.
Maybe you'd like to be a queen someday.
BWAHAHA HAHAHA!!
HAHA HAHAHA HAHAHAHA

What's so funny?
Can you imagine if I married you AND your sister?
What?
Congratulations to our parents! Sebastian's a two for one deal!
Wait, what? What about Sebastian?
SWOON

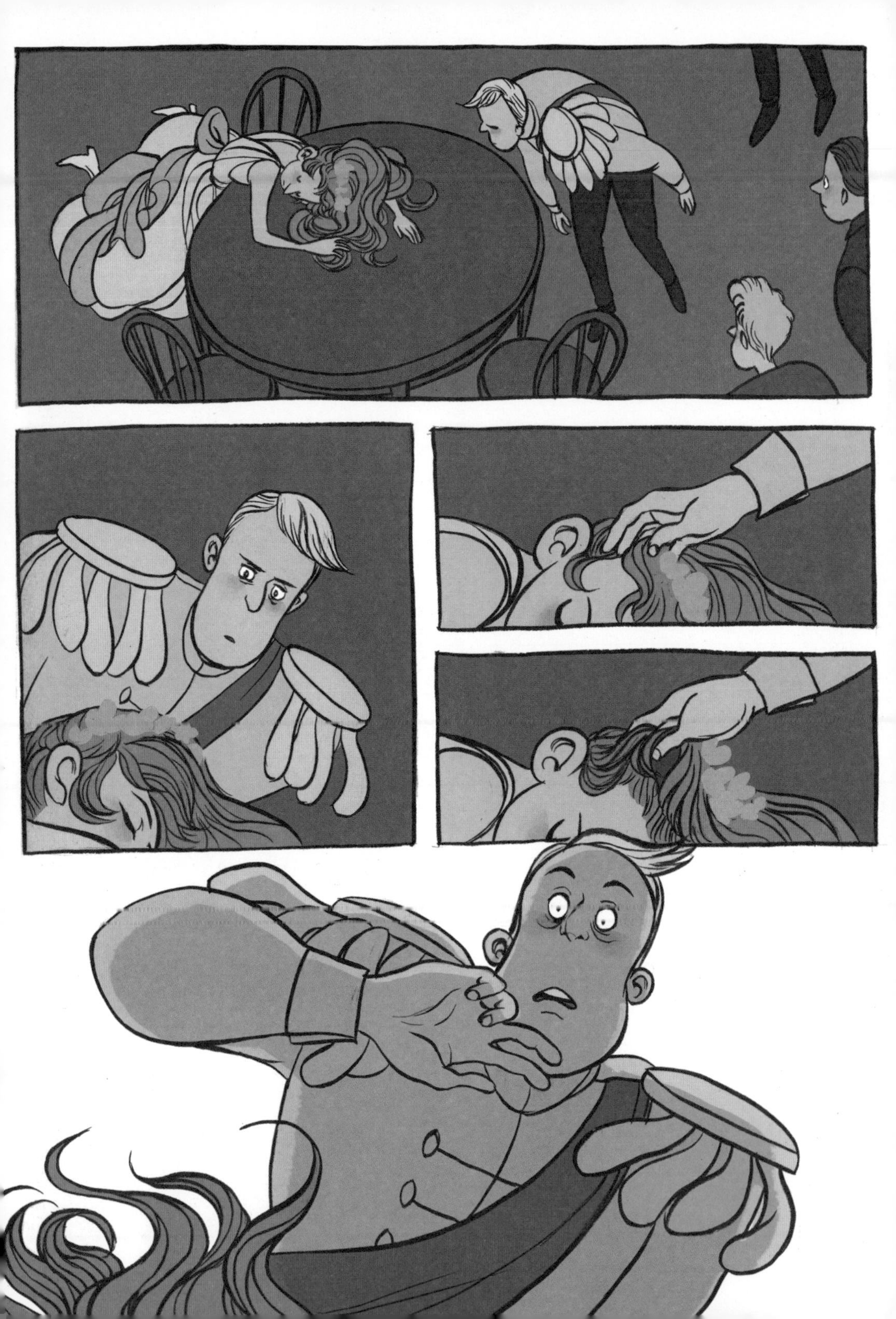

what happens now?

We have to hide him. Pick him up.
PICK HIM UP.
We'll deal with Juliana later. Right now no one can know about this.

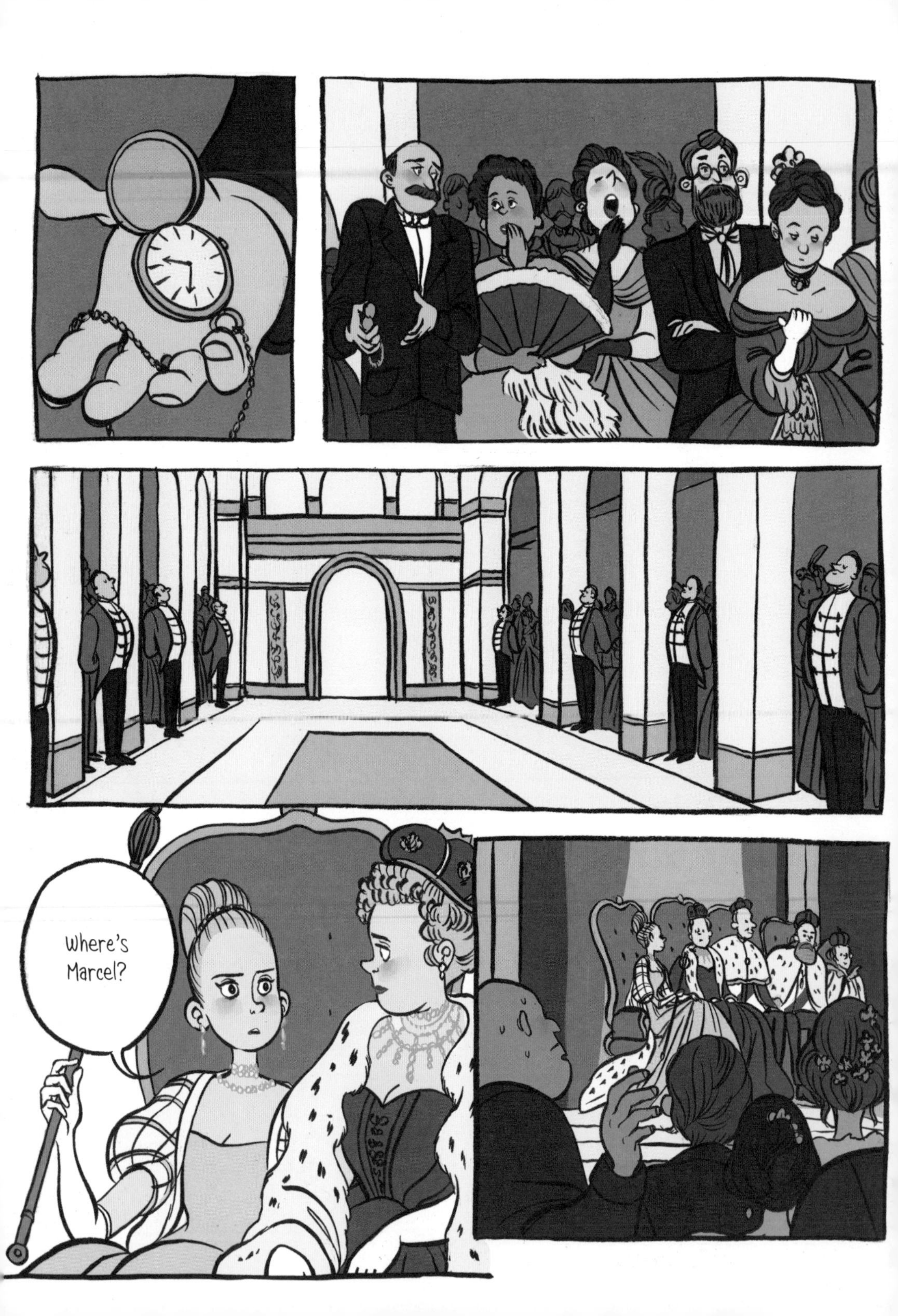
Where's
Marcel?

Your Highness, I've looked everywhere. He is nowhere to be found.
Well, what the bloody hell could he possibly be doing?
I will keep looking.
Your Highness, the truth is Sebastian requested to go out last night and I obliged him. He never returned.
Oh, for goodness sake...
Your Highness, I apologize—
Nevermind, nevermind. We'll deal with this.

Your attention, ladies and gentlemen! Our prince is running late today so we will proceed with the ceremony without him.
Princess Juliana, if you could step up here, please.
STOP!

We found your prince.

That's Lady Crystallia! Marcel, what are you doing?!
Take a closer look.

What is this? What are you doing with my son?
Your Highness, I found your son last night at the music hall. Except at first I didn't realize it was him.
He was dressed like this.

Calls himself LADY Crystallia. I think he's the one you should be asking questions.
Crystallia. This whole time, it was you?
Leroy, that's my dress! The dress that's been missing all these years!
How long has this been going on?

A very long time. I'm sorry.
I can't do this.

Mother?
Father?

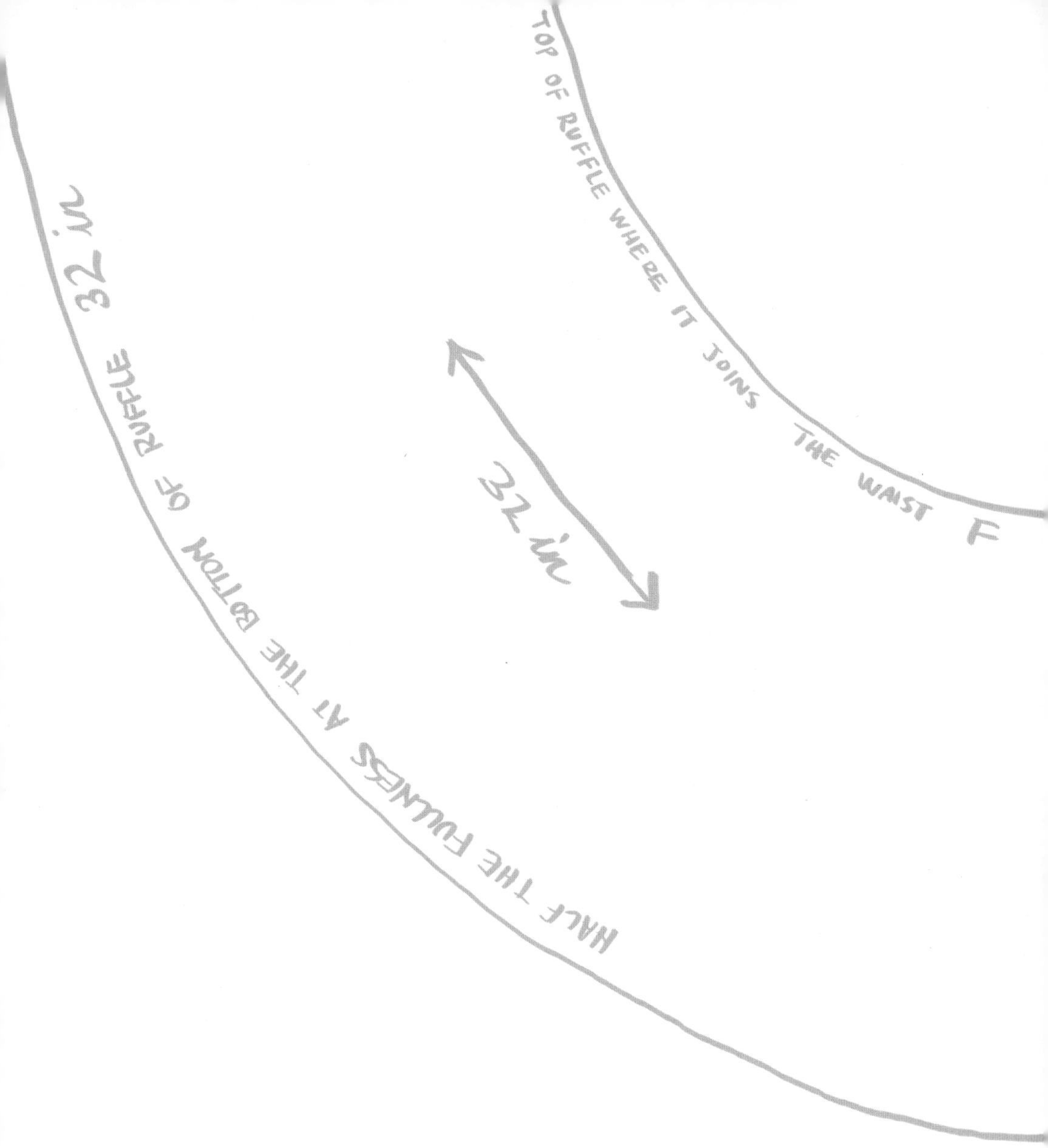

TOP OF RUFFLE WHERE IT JOINS THE WAIST F

32 in

32 in

HALF THE FULLNESS AT THE BOTTOM OF RUFFLE

Chapter 10

And just like that, he admits he's been dressing up as a girl this whole time!
That's amazing!

All those girls who've been throwing themselves at him must feel like such idiots right now.
AND I hear he was wearing his mother's dress when they caught him, too.
BWAHAHAHA HAHAHAH!!
SLAM

You monsters.

Emile!

What happened? Please tell me he's okay.
Sebastian is gone. He told everyone the truth.
Where did he go?
He ran off.
I don't know where. The King and queen are preparing to head back to Brussels. I am to stay here in case I hear of anything.
Sebastian did make one request to me the night before the party. He put away all the clothes you made for him.
He wanted you to have them.

What are
you doing
here?

I know who you are. You're the seamstress. You made all his...
Your Highness. I was Prince Sebastian's personal—
...garments.
How did this happen? What did I do wrong?

Nothing, Your Highness. All he ever wanted was to please you and your wife. This is the way he is.
Do you know where my son is?
No.
If I may, Your Highness.

A number of these items belong to the queen. You should take them back.
How could I have missed all the signs?
If you know so much about my son, why was he confused about himself? What was he missing?

No, Your Highness. He wasn't confused about himself. The thing that ruined Sebastian was how afraid he was of what you'd think of him.
What you DO think of him.
He was perfect.
Emile

I have to admit, I'm not very good at this lifestyle. I didn't know I'd have to do so much gardening.
How're my parents?
They're coping. They're on their way back to Brussels.
Why did you decide to contact me?
I've written some apology letters I'd like you to deliver.
Julian

There are ones for my parents, for Juliana...
...for Frances...
Frances
I was able to deliver your clothes to Frances.
How is she?
She's doing well. She's found employement with George Trippley's son.
Peter? Where? The department store?
She said she was working on a fashion show.
Oh.

If you don't need anything else, I should be on my way. Your parents will want to know you're safe and well.
Are you going to be all right?
Yes.

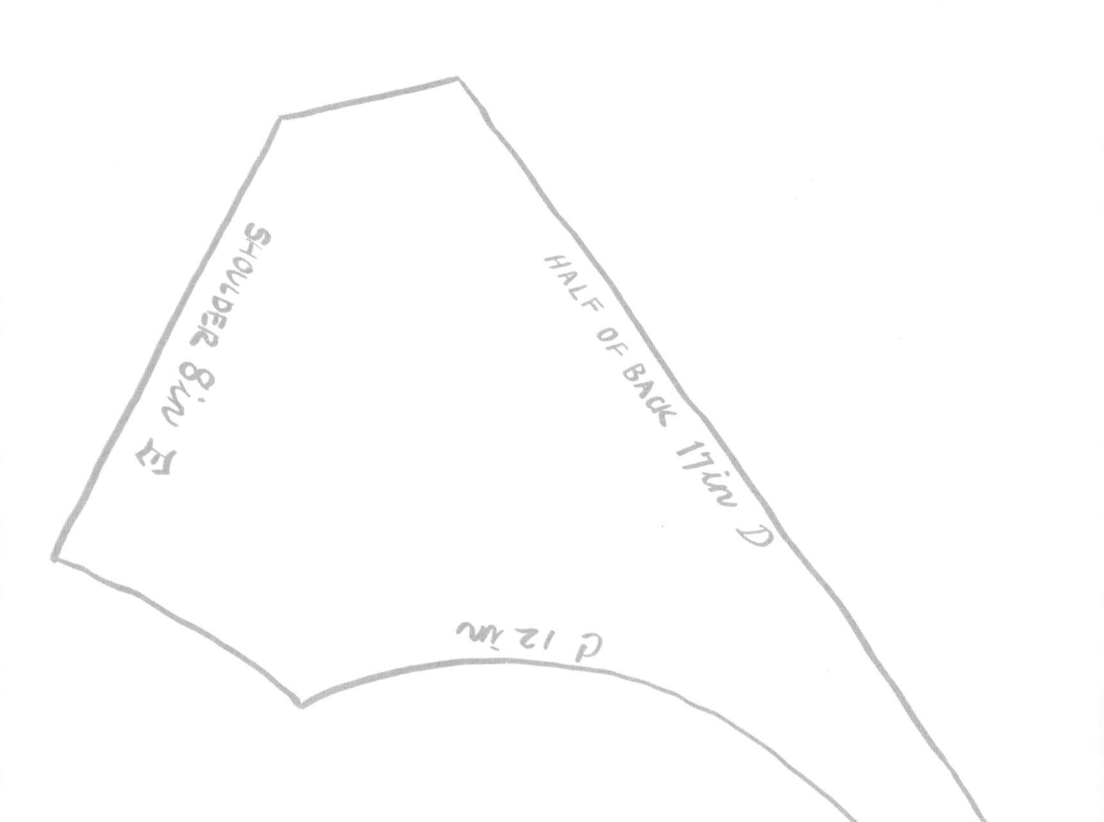

Chapter 11

You look lovely.
Thank you.
The collection is perfect.
It's elegant. It's classic. They're the perfect outfits for the sophisticated shopper we're trying to court.
See, all you needed was a little guidance.
Now you're going to be a star, Frances.

What's wrong?
Oh, nothing. Thank you for everything, Peter. This is a dream come true.
KNOCK
KNOCK
Are we ready to move, sir?
Of course. Come on in.
Good luck, Frances. I'll see you upstairs.

Ladies and gentlemen, you are part of a historic occasion! Welcome to the grand opening of Trippley's!
To celebrate, we've put together a special treat for you. Prepare to witness the next evolution in fashion!
Maestro!

Hey!

SEBASTIAN!

Ssh!
What are you doing here?!
Emile told me everything.
I wanted to come see your show.

Peter loves it. He says it's exactly what his shoppers want.
Is this what YOU want?
Yes! This is my dream come true. All of it!
Is it, though? Your name is on the dress but the dress has none of you in it!

People's tastes can change.
That's what I used to tell myself, too.
This isn't about you, Sebastian.
I make the decisions now, and this is what I've decided to be.

I'm happy your dreams are coming true. Good luck out there.
The trunk.

With the collection I made for you and Aurelia.
I never got rid of it. It's in the studio downstairs.
Yeah?
There's still time to get the models changed.
Help me?

There's your prince.
Mother! Father!

My son! I've been so worried about you!
How could we leave without you!
If it weren't for Emile, we wouldn't have known you were even alive!
I thought you all went back to Brussels?

Thirty minutes to stage, Frances.
Mother, I'm sorry I never told you the truth. But this is who I am.
I'm a prince who likes dresses.
Father. If you're here to take me home, I'll go willingly. I just request that we wait until the show is over.

I'm not here to embarrass you, I'm just here to support Frances. She needs my help. Please.
Men?
Yessir!
You are going to help the prince and the dressmaker any way you can. See to their needs.
Yes, sir!
Come. We don't have much time.

And now, ladies and gentlemen, may I present to you a new collection by a very young, very exciting new designer, debuting a sophisticated new women's collection! Here it is!
Maestro!

What's going on back here?
You! You're that prince! Of course this is your doing!
Grab him!

Sebastian!
Frances!
Get them out of here. I'm taking my show back!
No, you are not.

Get your hands off my child.
Who're you? I'm the owner of this building!
And I'm the king.

This show will go on exactly as they please.
Now if you'll excuse me, it's my turn to take the stage.

I can't believe that's my father out there.

Why are you doing all this for us?
Look around. In a world where department stores exist, where do kings and princes even fit in anymore?
When I first learned the truth, I thought Sebastian's life would be ruined. But seeing you, I realized everything would be fine.
Because someone still loved him.

My friend, Frances.
Allow me to introduce the designer:

Hey. That wasn't too bad. Well done, Frances.
Not what I was expecting, of course, but the people really seem to like it.
And that's your best look yet, Crystallia.
Thanks, Peter.
See, I thought I recognized you. You should've told me you were the designer! That was fantastic.

Madame Aurelia. Nice to meet you.
I'm Frances.
I've been wanting to meet you for a very long time.

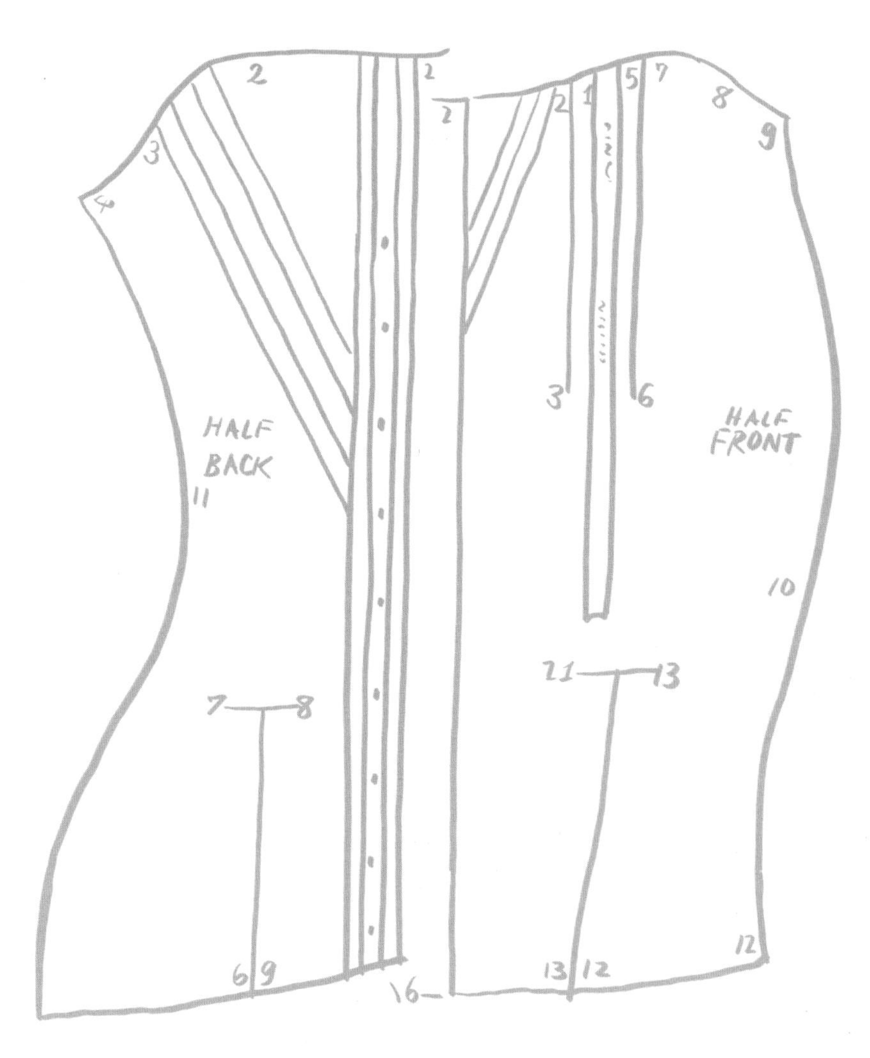

Chapter 12

Your Highness?
Pardon me for interrupting your studies. Your parents sent you a telegram. Shall I give you the message?
Yes, please!
They're wondering when you might be visiting Brussels next.

They miss you and hope your studies are going well. Also that you're not troubling your aunt too much.
Thank you, Emile. Tell them I'll come visit in a few weeks for my mother's birthday.
Also, my studies are going very well, and Aunt Clem and I are starting our own tennis club soon.
Very well. I will see to that.
Oh, and Emile...
Tell them I miss them, too.

Atelier de Aurelia

I have some new designs I want to show you.
Fin

My Process

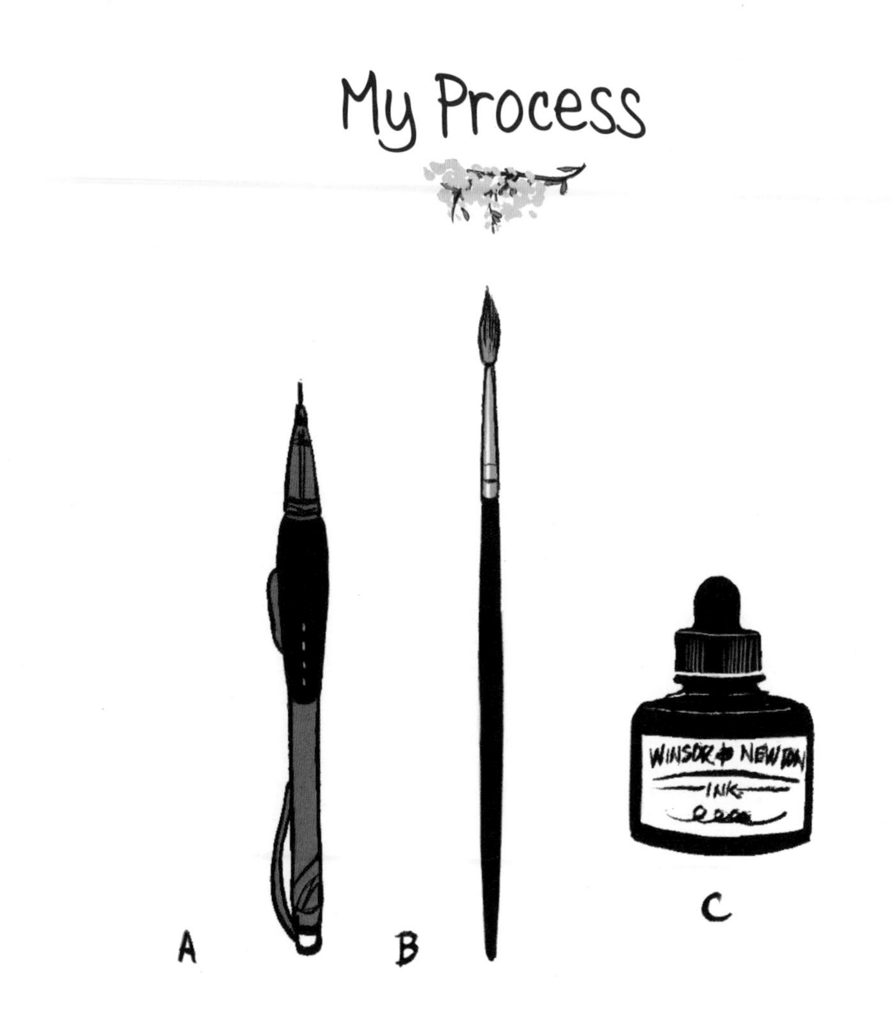

A) I draw with a mechanical pencil, 0.7 lead.
Any pencil will do. I've had this one for six years!

B) Winsor & Newton Series 7 Kolinsky Sable Brush, size 2.
This is what I ink with. I went through about two
of these brushes for this book.

C) Winsor & Newton ink. Inked with black india ink.

The first stage of book is the script! I write everything out beforehand so I can read it over and make changes I think will make the story better.

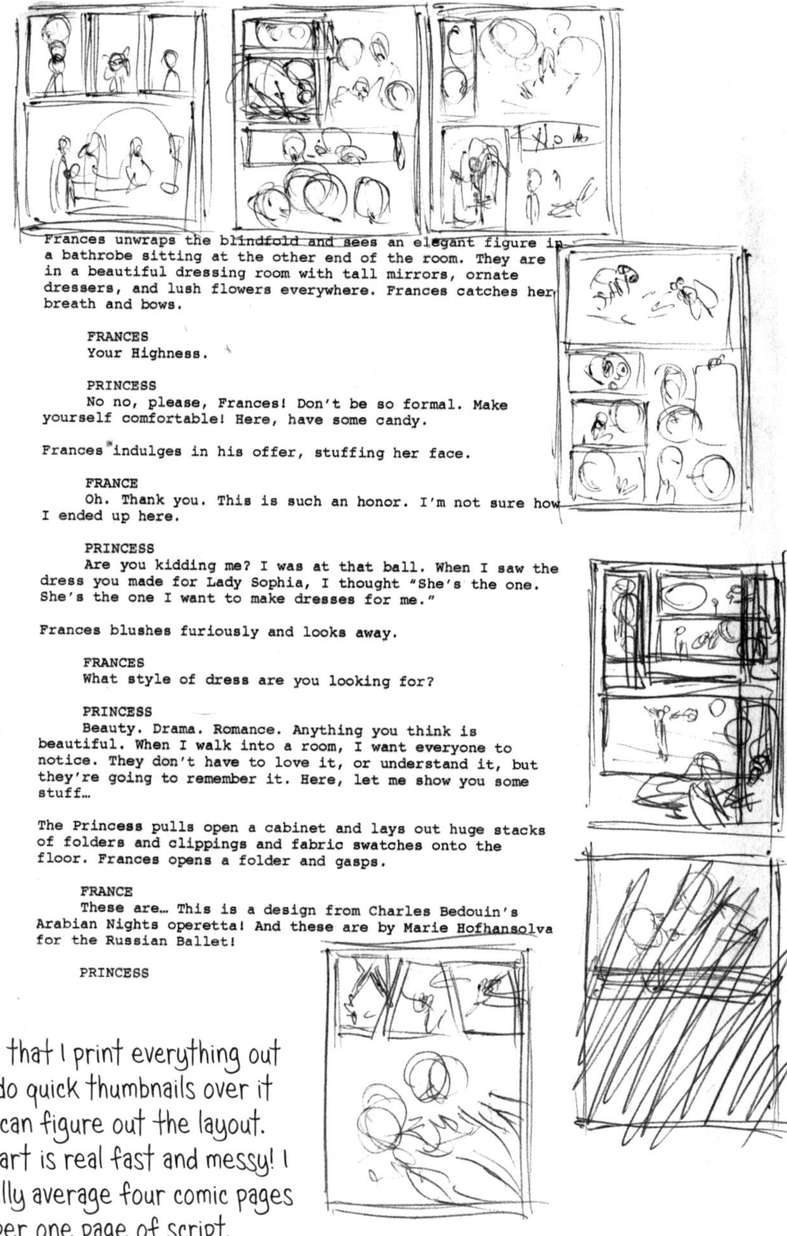

Frances unwraps the blindfold and sees an elegant figure in a bathrobe sitting at the other end of the room. They are in a beautiful dressing room with tall mirrors, ornate dressers, and lush flowers everywhere. Frances catches her breath and bows.

FRANCES
Your Highness.

PRINCESS
No no, please, Frances! Don't be so formal. Make yourself comfortable! Here, have some candy.

Frances indulges in his offer, stuffing her face.

FRANCE
Oh. Thank you. This is such an honor. I'm not sure how I ended up here.

PRINCESS
Are you kidding me? I was at that ball. When I saw the dress you made for Lady Sophia, I thought "She's the one. She's the one I want to make dresses for me."

Frances blushes furiously and looks away.

FRANCES
What style of dress are you looking for?

PRINCESS
Beauty. Drama. Romance. Anything you think is beautiful. When I walk into a room, I want everyone to notice. They don't have to love it, or understand it, but they're going to remember it. Here, let me show you some stuff…

The Princess pulls open a cabinet and lays out huge stacks of folders and clippings and fabric swatches onto the floor. Frances opens a folder and gasps.

FRANCE
These are… This is a design from Charles Bedouin's Arabian Nights operetta! And these are by Marie Hofhansolva for the Russian Ballet!

PRINCESS

After that I print everything out and do quick thumbnails over it so I can figure out the layout. This part is real fast and messy! I generally average four comic pages per one page of script.

Next is the penciling, which is done on 9" x 12" bristol paper.

Even though I already scripted the story, this is where the comic really starts to feel alive!

Drawing the characters as they go through the events, you can really feel their joys and sorrows, and it's the process I connect with the most.

Originally when I came up with the story, I imagined Sebastian and Frances as adults.

Here are two versions of an early sample comic I did, one with the characters as adults and the other as teenagers.

I decided on teenagers since very little of the story changed except that everything was heightened; the protagonists were discovering things about themselves for the first time, which made it more innocent and emotional.

I didn't have a lot of time to do detailed location and costume designs for every scene, so I would do quick sketches in between comic pages.

Here's a sketch that became the blueprint for Sebastian's room.

Published by First Second
First Second is an imprint of Roaring Brook Press, a division of
Holtzbrinck Publishing Holdings Limited Partnership
175 Fifth Avenue, New York, NY 10010

Library of Congress Control Number: 2017941173

Hardcover ISBN: 978-1-250-15985-4
Paperback ISBN: 978-1-62672-363-4

Our books may be purchased in bulk for promotional, educational, or business use.
Please contact your local bookseller or the Macmillan Corporate and Premium Sales Department
at (800) 221-7945 ext. 5442 or by e-mail at MacmillanSpecialMarkets@macmillan.com.

First edition 2018
Book design by Andrew Arnold and Taylor Esposito
Printed in China

Penciled with mechanical #2 pencil, inked with sable kolinsky brush and india ink, and colored digitally in Photoshop.

Hardcover: 10 9 8 7 6 5 4
Paperback: 10 9 8 7

BY ART WE LIVE